EL JEFE EN AZTLÁN

The Salinas Trilogy:

Book One: *Culpa de Sangre (Blood Guilt)*
Book Two: *El Jefe en Aztlán*
Book Three: *Madre*

Also by Robert Franklin Gish from Sunstone Press

Twilight Troubadour

EL JEFE EN AZTLÁN

AN ANIMAL'S QUEST FOR HOME

Second in the Salinas Trilogy

Robert Franklin Gish

SUNSTONE PRESS

SANTA FE

Sunstone books may be purchased for educational, business, or sales promotional use.
For information please write: Special Markets Department, Sunstone Press,
P.O. Box 2321, Santa Fe, New Mexico 87504-2321.
Printed on acid-free paper

eBook 978-1-61139-675-1

Library of Congress Cataloging-in-Publication Data

Names: Gish, Robert, author. | Gish, Robert Salinas trilogy ; 2nd.
Title: El Jefe en Aztlán : an animal's quest for home / Robert Franklin
  Gish.
Description: Santa Fe : Sunstone Press, [2022] | Series: Second in the
  Salinas Trilogy | Summary: "A phantom jaguar, known for god-like powers,
  returns to his mythical Chicano homeland of Aztlán intersecting and
  championing those in need"-- Provided by publisher.
Identifiers: LCCN 2022004926 | ISBN 9781632933812 (paperback) | ISBN
  9781611396751 (epub)
Subjects: LCSH: Animal ghosts--New Mexico--Fiction. | LCGFT: Magic realist
  fiction.
Classification: LCC PS3557.I79 J44 2022 | DDC 813/.54--dc23/eng/20220305
LC record available at https://lccn.loc.gov/2022004926

WWW.SUNSTONEPRESS.COM
SUNSTONE PRESS / POST OFFICE BOX 2321 / SANTA FE, NM 87504-2321 /USA
(505) 988-4418 / FAX (505) 988-1025

This narrative is a work of fiction and should be read as such—the product of the author's imagination while toying with Magical Realism. Its "truths" are *fictive* truths, strange as they might be. History, biography, and reality are something else to ponder. Which is to say that the characters and events found here, albeit compelling, are indeed imaginary.

"But species boundaries are, if not illusory, certainly vague and sometimes porous. Ask any evolutionary biologist or shaman."
—Charles Foster, *Being a Beast*

"Oh, la...le pauvre!
I shall run before him,
With a curious puffing.
He will bend his ear then.
I shall whisper
Heavenly labials in a world of gutturals.
It will undo him."
—Wallace Stevens, "The Plot Against the Giant"

"This [beast] has the shape of a lioness, but it is taller in the leg and slimmer and longer and quite white, marked with black spots after the manner of rosettes; all the animals are fascinated by these as they gaze at them and they would remain standing there always if it were not for the terror of its face; being conscious of this therefore it hides its face, and the animals that are round about it take courage and draw near for as to be able the better to enjoy so much beauty; it then suddenly seizes on the nearest and instantly devours it."
—Leonardo da Vinci, *Bestiary*

"The miracle is always there...for the man who can pass his hand through to it, to take it."
—D.H. Lawrence, *The Plumed Serpent*

"And you will remain with them
locked forever inside yourself
your eyes will see you
dark shaggy thick."
—Leslie Silko, "Story from Bear Country"

CONTENTS

ACKNOWLEDGEMENTS

My California *hermanos en construyendo la plan de estudios multicultural* did much in leading me toward my own personal discovery of Aztlán. So here's to the determination and persuasion of Pedro Arroyo, Refujio (Cuco) Rodriguez, and Hector Alvarez. And to M.E.Ch.A., especially the "fuse lighting "dedicated members at Cal Poly San Luiz Obispo who helped light the fire in developing Ethnic Studies there and who much sought after and lobbied for courses in Mexican American and Chicano Studies. Gratitude *y abrazos* also go out to Professor Victor Valle, his scholarship and general collegiality.

When it comes to increasing my knowledge of and familiarity with the wildlife of New Mexico and the Rocky Mountains, my long-time friend Richard Ray brought me back to my urban senses after leaving me alone with his Dutch oven and two bear hounds deep in the Gila Wilderness when he hoofed his solo way to Magdalena to find a replacement distributor for our disabled pickup.

Spending such a time alone, especially at night, awakens you to the truths of Leslie Silko's poetic account of human/bear metamorphosis. My beloved wife, Judith, continues to dispel any such loneliness with her own brand of bear hugs.

Special thanks go out to guitarists Vince Lewis and Frank Potenza. Their music keeps me *jazzed* up, remembering that EGBDF (i.e., every good boy does fine) if you FACE (i.e., face) the music enchanted and in tune.

ABG Allen's suggestions brought more focus to the structure of the story. And Mr. Daniel R. Butzier enabled the more difficult electronic aspects of writing.

I dedicate this book again with abiding affection to AKC who inspires me, forever bringing meaning to "Cathexis."

(N.B.: Some poetic license is required here in that the author at times speaks through me, El Jefe, a jaguar, only to emphasize that animals and authors oftentimes merge in their story telling.)

PROLOGUE

I've never put as much faith in words as I do in sounds. Words are at once too limiting and precise and yet too vague and general. Although my vocabulary is as vast as a god's should be, I don't belabor words as such, although I can translate, rather understand, several languages, including that of indigenous peoples and, of course, as an animal I know hand signs and sign languages. Don't get me wrong. I'm no Were-jaguar. No 'therianthrope.' Well, maybe. I'll leave the final determination up to you and, given my diachronic, trans-temporal and shapeshifting tendencies, to the story. Trust the tale not the teller D.H. Lawrence advises.

Admittedly, words and their sounds do carry meanings and tones and, as such, are open to variable as maps and designated places, territories and ranges, situations and habitats, ecology and climatic zones, seasons and freedom and control and ownership and government and laws and agencies and actors—both good and bad, suggesting morality, ethics, what's right and what's wrong and according to whom, for whom and for what. More muddledom you say. And you're right. Everything's more complicated than it seems and relative to the "seemer," or "schemer."

It's important, however, for you, my audience, to think about such things, about relativity and complexity, not just subtlety and nuance but magic (magical realism as it were) if you want to really grasp this story or rather these narratives. In any brave new world you pays your money and you takes your choice; you gotta buy the premise pard, suspend your disbelief. Forget about realism, verisimilitude, unity, and all that. Remember people paid good money to go see "Cat People," that eight-million-dollar rotten tomato. Or read Blake's "The Tyger," or T.S. Eliot's cat poems, or W. B. Yeats or read Van Tilburg Clark's *Track of the Cat*, or Poe's "The Black Cat," or Hemingway's "Short Happy Life of Francis Macomber." Or Andrew Lloyd Webber, or…. You get the gist. We dominate these stories.

Here we're all about a larger story about a real and imagined place and a myth known as "Aztlán," and about me, *El Jefe*, a legendary, real yet mythical jaguar, a supreme hunter, a premier prowler known and named in the present iteration by a children's school contest as "The Chief." Not so much the king of the jungle but the chief, the boss of the mountains. It's about my passage, *señor* and *señora*, *y mi presencia en Aztlán*, both the place and the belief, the idea, or mind map that ranges from Guatemala to Guaymas, from Mexico City to Tucson, from Mesoamerica to the present American Southwest and the Gila and Manzano mountains of New Mexico. Just part of the nominal known. Just names. And landmarks. Spirits, however, do rest in places say the anthropologists.

My ancestry, real and imagined, is old. Some have called me "Lord of the Dark," the night stalker, and "He who kills with one blow." But that involves translations from Nuatal, Spanish, and Tewa and other indigenous languages, cultures who see me as a god. As for the cosmopolitan Brits, they've named a classy car for me. Go figure, old chap! My existence isn't dependent on culture or history so much as it is on biology and how I fit into the knowns and unknowns of taxonomy. Aztlán exists without me, of course, just as do Mexico and South America, names on maps, lines of fabricated boundaries determined by wars and surveys and purchases and theft.

My existence, my evolution and biology, admittedly heighten the allure, the mystique, and the exoticism associated with jungles, wilderness and the wild…the sublime and the beautiful. Questions about the fearful symmetry of the tiger, and the hand and eye responsible for it might also be asked about me. Why the spots? Where the spots? Superficial or skin deep? How related to the tiger, the panther, the cheetah, the puma, leopard, the lynx, the ocelot, even the half-tame domestic cat? Dog and cat might be the first words some children learn but its an obvious over-simplification of the feline typology. *Todos son mi gente. Esé Carnal! Qué vive La Raza!*

In contemporary times the notion of Aztlán is associated with politics and the Chicano movement of the mid to late twentieth century as an ancient myth of the promised land, a kind of El Dorado, marking the American Southwest as the home of *Los Indios* who migrated north to the central valley of Mexico and further north to what became states known as New Mexico and Arizona in my father's time of 1912. Just the other day, as it were, for my kin.

Call me cat. Call me *El Gato*. Call me Chicano. Call me predator. Call me hungry. Call me Jaguar! *Yo soy El Jefe!* And I am going along, and so is my story…. People can't seem to stop talking about me or searching me out for their nearsighted, homocentric, murderous, almost universally pernicious reasons. If I could only rewrite Genesis as read by *Los Cristianos*, the Christian world. In my rewrite animals might be said to rule as we actually have and still do if only in the names of football, baseball, and basketball teams. How about a shout out for the Carolina Panthers, the Detroit Lions, the Cincinnati Bengals, and, of course, the Jacksonville Jaguars. And so, *vamanos gente*, grab me by the tale tail and hang on. Here we go…*Vamos a Aztlán, la tierra de mi alma*."

1
LA NOCHE

"Darkness. Finally. Moon. Bright. Nightlight. Seeing beyond the shadows. Around the shadows. Through the shadows. The shadows. Colores. Favorites. Deer. The crossing. Kill hunger. Kill fast. Death...comes. Shadows follow. Hiding shadow...Lunge. Black. Devour. Silence. It comes."

El Jeffe, a stranger in a strange yet familiar land, had travelled north for many months, stalking his prey, hungry for meat, for his destiny, pulled by it, a haunting memory eating at him, drawn by it as much as by hunger, throughout the days into the nights, through heat, through cold, now even more tired and even more famished than after his last kill. Today his hunger had taken longer. From dusk until now. But the moon was brighter and he had exhausted his prey, following it to his preferred striking place.

Here. This night. Now.

He would spring for the neck first and fast. Even if he missed the vein, his still blood-stained claws would hold and bring down the animal, holding fast to the creature's back. Tonight the meal was again venison, though he knew the taste, not that name. He knew the spiked horns would prevent a strike to the back of the skull. So the neck. The blood. The taste. Tasty young deer trying in vain to evade Jefe's wiles.

The new yet worn and familiar paths were known to him by instinct, sight, yes, feel and smell—remembered earth travelled by others too, like the generations of *la gente,* like his kin ocelot and puma, and padded-patted down, paw after paw, marked with urine. Familiar in smell. The deer would be here. Better than birds. Better than peccary. Better than turtle. And snake. Better than racoon. Hunger would soon be satisfied. Here very soon. Ah, but thirst! The stream was still near. For that he was grateful.

There! Now! He must strike fast avoiding the other larger deer. Get the young one. Now! He sprang and his growling cry and its accompanying, gurgling scream rang through the canyons, carrying along and across the foothills down to the llano, the ranch, and the town. Terrorizing the cattle and sheep and sending chills through the people now checking their guns.

Raul and his wife turned in their sleep. Their dogs growled low and raised their heads in the direction of the sounds of blood and death. Cattle stopped their relentless chewing. The sheep huddled closer in their pasture and pens.

El Jefe had arrived. El Jefe, still believing *La Union hace la fuerza*, had returned to Aztlán.

2
La Peluqueria

Saturday was a busy day for Samson "Shorty" Sisneros at his Main Street barbershop "The Razor's Den" in Mountainair, New Mexico. Sunday and Monday he was closed. Through the week few could leave their farms and ranches, school, or business unattended. Besides, Saturday was the time and Shorty's the place for a no-holds-barred gabfest of news, *chistes*, *charlando*, and local gossip. Shorty had bold-lettered signs on the shop walls saying things like "Haircut While You Wait," "*Cortolo la caca!*" "Cut it short, cut it out, but cut it." "Look your best when you feel your worst." Shorty had a thing for *dichos* and wall sayings—all painted in barber-pole colors. The irony of it all was his name and his extreme comb-over, the longest strands of which he bleached with peroxide every night after closing.

His barbering license hung prominently in its prideful place, over the mirror behind his first-chair spot. He wasn't big on jokes, especially dirty ones like some ear-whispering barbers who think it's an expected part of the trade. No, Shorty was a serious fellow, a mason, a member of the Pentecostal church when with a pastor, and the Mountainair Chamber of Commerce. He never missed a Lions Club meeting or a Saturday pancake benefit.

Samson thought of himself as a stalwart. A community leader! A photograph of him in his red Shriner fez hung as a centerpiece just over his large mirror (its corner boasting his first ten-dollar tip) where he turned his customers to check out the result of his clipping and scissoring, always saying, "*Que guapo*! That's one *suave* job, *hermano*!" He hummed "*Mi Cafetal*" in ecstasy when it came time to apply the hot, foamy, lather and shave around his customers' ears—imagining a *misto caliente* scorching his taste buds.

Shorty's anorexic son, Manuel "Shaggy" Sisneros, was everything Shorty was not. Did it bother Shorty that his *flaco* son liked his hair long and shaggy like the Biblical Samson—thus the hirsute nickname? That he wore extension nails? Sure thing! Shorty hated longhair (even his own comb over) and long fingernails as much as Manuel loved them. Just about all Manny ever did was hang out in the shop's back room, arrange his bottles of fingernail hardener and colors from pink to purple, blue to brown, and clip and file and polish his fingernails. By paying such attention to his own hands, he'd developed into a tolerable, manicurist and had asked his father countless times if he could set up a table equipped with emery boards, a virtual cornucopia of corundum, delicate files and scissors, in the front of the shop—just a small table, a lamp, and two chairs. He kept his multiple tools of the trade in a carryall for house calls if they ever came.

As it was, he was sequestered away, stuck behind a curtain which slid open only when by some oddity a customer asked for a manicure—a request which took a lot of courage in the small town where men were men and women were women and Manuel was queer, unlike most in Bob Hope's "Buttons and Bows" Western parody.

The third accomplice in Shorty's "cut it short; not shaggy" shop was Henry "Chrome Dome" Lewis, the tall and muscular Black shine "boy," though no one really knew his name or age for sure, but his head was as bald as the proverbial billiard ball or in this case a trailer hitch, thus the shiny nickname. With his tall, lumbering physique and overrun, over-sized scuffed brogues, lumbering gait and tonsured gray hair he certainly wasn't a "boy." All anyone thought about was that he had a drinking problem and he could give a hell of a spit shine and pop that Chattanooga shine cloth like a towel in a school locker room.

Carlos Muñoz said that he's seen Henry in the YMCA pool shower, and vowed Henry's endowments would put anyone to shame. Henry mumbled a lot and word was that when he escaped the Tulsa race riots back in 1921 he headed "out West" to lose himself and the mob rule prejudice and leg injury he'd suffered, landing mysteriously on Shorty's doorstep. Only Henry and those who lingered to read the barber license knew that Shorty's certificate from the Tulsa Barber College was dated the very year of the rioting.

Everyone called Henry's boss "Shorty," if on his good side, not because he wasn't well hung like Henry but because he was one short guy—so short he had to stand on a small footstool painted red, white and blue to ply his trade. First-time customers were rare, in part because his was the only place to get a haircut or a shave in the small farming and sheep town at the western edge of the Manzano Mountains.

You could travel for a haircut, drive into the city, be it Socorro or Belen to the north, or even further north to Albuquerque, the Duke City, so named for its Spanish founder The Duke of Albuquerque. Some did make that trip, but only the particular, only the singular and the vain, only the fastidious, the latter in short supply in that small-town and surrounding locale.

This particular Saturday the place was full. Summer was all but over and autumn and its rituals and events were underway: school was starting, weddings, funerals, box suppers, and hunting season were in the offing all heading into Thanksgiving and Christmas. A town picnic was planned for Labor Day and a country band called "Billy Wheeler and the Hubcaps" was headlined to play in the pavilion and that was somewhat controversial since the town of Truth of Consequences (formerly Hot Springs because of its mineral baths), home town of the band, was an arch rival of the Mountainair Monarchs. There might be a "rumble" was the word from teen world.

Raul entered the Razor's Den, tossed his dusty and sweaty Resistol, broad-brimmed cowboy hat on the rack by the door and asked "How long a wait, Shorty?" "*Diez minutos, hermano*, or shorter," he chuckled, "like everything in this "*aqui y ahora*" short cut establishment. Let me finish up with Celso and you're next after Ernesto over there with Henry, shining those worthless, overrun boots.

Manuel walked over to sit by Raul to say hello and ask, "*Que pasa Don Guapo?* How's the great brown hunter and guide? Ready for the season with those Texans wanting to kill all our deer? Antonio Marez was in here earlier saying he'd come across a dead buck up high country by *Manzano* Peak, pretty much eaten up by a mountain lion. He said he found a couple of hairballs. And cat tracks were everywhere, he said."

"Yeah, boss, Henry spoke up, lots of customers talking about mountain lions or big bob cats. Reuben Abeyta said he's lost some cattle, finding only a carcass or two at his eastern line."

Celso, just getting out of Shorty's chair, glanced again in the mirror while observing to Raul and the others, that he had seen something cat-like the other night, when driving the side road to his ranch, that looked more like a panther than a lion, but it was fast, very fast and soon loped out of sight. *Quisas una poblema puma*! He reported calling Roscoe Powers the next day at Elephant Butte Game and Fish, who said reports were coming in from further south of a spotted, sometimes black lion, probably a jaguar ranging out of its territory, and they were investigating.

"Get real, Simón chimed in. No one drives a Jaguar in these parts, new or vintage!"

"*Que tonto Váto,*" Shorty muttered. Not a car but a cat, a real big fast cat! Almost as fast as his *primo* Cheetah."

Finally Raul said in a loud voice, "Okay, okay, guys, get a grip. These stories are exaggerations, there hasn't been a jaguar this far north in generations. Not here in New Mexico at least. They're part of myth, stories told by the old ones about an animal god from across the border, from the Aztecs and the Incas. Myths! Old attempts at explaining God and his ways. Pretty soon we'll be talking about human sacrifice and cutting out the hearts of virgins. "*Hay, Sagrado Corazón,*" he whispered, crossed himself, and kissed his worn Saint Francis necklace.

Soon after getting his hair cut and what Shorty called "getting his ears lowered," Raul headed for his Ram 1500 diesel pickup, at first confusing the grill for an F-150 the same color, all the while remembering the unearthly roar he and his family had heard nights before, causing him to grab his pistol and go outside and check on the dogs, walk around the barn and take a look inside at some of his penned up, agitated sheep.

"Come back for a manicure or a facial, *Señor* Raul," Manny yelled down the street to him, waving a frenzied, loose-wristed goodbye. Raul brushed some hair off his collar and raised his hand in a half-hearted wave, resolved to give old Roscoe Powers a call, if the reprobate would answer having argued with Raul over one of last year's Texan blowhards' license and tag fee. "Better clear up this jaguar business before they come again this fall," Raul mused.

3
MANOS DE ORO

Nina looked down at her hands, wondering where they got their strength. Where she got the strength, especially this late in the day. One of her clients, Ted Waxman, after his appointment, had brought her a caramel macchiato from the coffee shop next door. It was her favorite pick-me-up and Ted was a regular, a retired state cop who had a late-in-life codger crush on her. Each visit he brought her flowers or a bottle of wine (grape juice or *Mosto*, he called it, trying too hard to learn Spanish).

Felix Aguilar, the man tabled on his stomach, was her last client of the day—another policeman, this one an APD sergeant in the "violent crimes" division.

He was ambitious and advancing in the department. He was young, good looking—and overly flirtatious, telling her she still looked "hot." Little did she know his dark, buried life.

She let his inappropriate word slide for the moment, familiar with such attachments and seldom bothered by sexist and sexy compliments and comments. Dues meant more than words to her. Besides, she had a brother, loved the *machismo* of her father and her uncle, had put up with the deranged oddities of her first husband, and now knew the burgeoning, hormonal drives, bulges, and soiled clothing of teenage sons. Familiar with stealth clothing, Nina knew well enough not to wear her physical trainer attire when assuming her massage therapist role, changing from bright-colored, form-fitting leggings and tight tank tops into medical scrubs.

She didn't think of herself as "hot" but knew that now in her mid-thirties she was in great shape, still turned heads in stores and couldn't count the times she'd been complimented as "lovely," a term she preferred although "sexy" she had to admit still registered with her self-image. Her promotional photos on social media definitely gravitated toward that appraisal.

Nina was truly well proportioned and terrifically preserved. "Beautiful," in a word. Lovely green, dazzling eyes. Full, contoured lips made for kissing, without a hint of Botox augmentation. Most of her beauty was natural, thanks to Linda, her mother, being born with a lean, curvaceous body and a divine complexion, radiant hair countless people yearned for and fitness advertisements and products promoted. But she worked hard to preserve it, seeing herself as exemplary, being a physical trainer, and advocate of calisthenics, kettle bells, free weights, isometrics, and cardio drills. Her husband, Anthony Aruejo had designed a body-building and self-defense course especially for her, including mitts, batons, and even deadly weaponry. She boasted of no misshapen muscle-bound physique. All the muscles were in the right places and her skin was smooth, firm, tanned, inviting—almost irresistible to touch—painfully so by the likes of old Ted.

This marriage, her second, was good. Her now husband was good-natured, a gentleman, almost too much of one, which she attributed to his Filipino culture, but she loved him sincerely and was grateful for the opportunities of his gym. Her work as a trainer, and now her massage component had truly provided professional fulfillment. She had enjoyed the physical trainer and massage therapist certification processes, a "hand in glove" union she somewhat humorously had observed—all of it, the studying, her fellow students, even the exams. In brief, she liked her job and she liked men generally and felt she knew them. In a way, she sensed all men were adolescents susceptible to women as sister, saint, siren, and most of all in need of mothering.

Somehow the word was out and city and state cops were flocking to her for their stress, their guilt, their nightmares—especially first responders like Aguilar, ostensibly "investigating" Albuquerque's West Mesa murders, human trafficking, prostitution, and child pornography cases. They often, sometimes half asleep during their appointments, mumbled into the face ring about the trauma they had experienced. And their trauma Nina registered during the sessions, and carried home with deep and disturbing empathy.

Suddenly looking down and reflecting on her hands, slick and moist from the lotions she was using, her gold and turquoise wedding ring shown oily and iridescent in the soft, reflected light of the darkened massage room. Indian flute music was trance-like until she felt a trigger point in Aguilar's left shoulder, decorated with a whimsical tattoo of a toothsome Felix the Cat eating a tortured house mouse. Noticing that, and grimacing at it snapped her out of a disturbing reverie about her own past school-girl traumas and the pain and regret of having an elaborate tattoo of a Phoenix inked on her back, only recently removed. Her hands strangely had a mind of their own beyond muscle memory or schooling, maybe two or more minds—when to hold, when to press, when to release, when to wander, pat, caress, or linger. When to punch and burrow in with her elbow! When to slap, karate like.

Somehow, curiously, and disturbingly this client reminded her of one of the Crawford boys who had, with his brother, raped her years back there in her father's barn. Now the misting from the hissing humidifier seemed to come from the mouse caught in the open-mouth tattoo. That sound and the pungent oils in the small humidifier synchronized with her own suddenly heavy breathing. She consciously pushed sharp and hard with her elbow on the grotesque tattoo.

The man groaned, saying, "What the hell, woman? I felt that for sure. *El Gato* can bite back, *entendes?* You get mean with him and he'll get angry." The prone, now royally pissed man, rubbed his shoulder and, partially sitting up, readjusted himself on the table.

"Apologies," Nina said. That was a rough spot to work out," knowing that she had willingly applied harmful pressure. "I'll give you an extra few minutes to make up for it."

"Okay! Under the right conditions I could stay here all day," Aguilar said with zest, if you climb up here with me and taste my copcicle. Just a quick lick! *Soy Necessito un beso de una puta ahora!*"

"Whoa, mister! No talk like that here! You are

way out of line! Gross! Obscene! Professional rules and personal values find that kind of talk, totally offensive! Totally off limits! You crossed a very well-defined line. So time is up right now! And I won't be scheduling any more appointments for you."

Aguilar got up from the massage table with a quick jump and in the darkened room sprang up to grab Nina in a frantic shuffling of bare feet and flailing of arms. She retreated, her back hitting against the wall and partially throwing her off balance.

He caught her and held her by the shoulders, shaking her body so that her neck wobbled to-and-fro for a second or two before she was able to push him back and double back her fingers for a palm thrust to his nose. The sound of the cartilage breaking sounded like someone had dropped a 25-pound plate weight out in the gym.

Aguilar let out a roar and grabbed his face, whimpering *chingada mujer, me has roto la nariz.*"

Nina made a lurch to turn on the light and push open the door to rush into the sanctuary of the gym and whoever was still working out.

Nina, red-faced and flustered, stormed out the door and left the small, now blood-stained and defiled room.

Luckily, a couple of fitness members were training and spotting each other and she hurried over to talk, shaking, breathless words coming with them.

They noted right away something was wrong and that she was scratched. Her scrubs were blood-splattered and torn! "For God's sake, what happened, Nina? You need us to call the police? Anything we can do, we'll do it!"

"Just keep talking with me for a minute. I'm in shock. That bastard got physical with me. Let's just hope he's leaving now."

So the two men huddled around her a bit closer, asking about the blood and scratches on her neck, as Aguilar left the massage room, still spewing vulgarisms—his blood-soaked shirt covering his nose and face. Trying to carry his shoes, he hobbled toward the gym door. "That's not the last of this," he turned and mumbled to Nina in anger. "Not by a long shot. Just remember you're dealing with *la ley, la policia*! *Mucho ojo puta mujer! Watchate!*"

What did he say? Her two would-be protectors said, starting to go after him as he got in his un-marked but antenna-laden car.

~

Nina went back to her massage room and sat down at her small desk to try and compose herself. She unwrapped a lemon-honey lozenge and took down her account book, turning to the name of "Aguilar, Felix," she drew a heavy albeit shaky Sharpie line through it, noting, "Abusive incident. Dangerous client. Discontinue appointments. Talk to Anthony. Sean O'Toole and Jack Foley, witnessed his anger and threat."

She sucked hard on the sweet lozenge, swallowing the juices hoping that their medicinal qualities would steady her palsied hand. She thought again about how massage school had recommended, and established the strictures and rules of professional behavior on her part. But what about disruptive and insulting clients? Apparently, you couldn't even count on norms of civil, polite behavior by police. She would file a formal complaint at City Hall or somewhere. But what the "He said/She said," use? Her self-defense training surfaced in her mind, grateful she knew how to protect herself! She knew she had applied extra force subconsciously, inevitably, reacting to the tattoo and her own disturbing reverie. His nose? She intended to break it and more.

Almost reflexively she reached for her phone and called 311, the city's help line. The operator who answered turned out to be a ghost from the past.

"Hello, this is operator six-twelve Louise Cahill. How can I help you? After a few seconds pause and a gulp Nina said, "Louise? Louise Cahill? The cheerleader? This is Nina Lucero, you know, from Mountainair."

After some rapid catching up Nina told Louise

she needed to report an attack but was wary because the culprit was a city policeman.

"I'll put you through to the internal affairs officer, Captain Alice Cain. She'll be extra confidential. No fears. I'll fill her in on our past."

Nina nervously and cautiously briefed the I.A. officer, providing the name of the attacker and the details as she remembered them, saying matter-of-factly, "I fear his reprisals." Cain said little in reply other than she would look into it and file a contact report.

Nina thanked the officer and said goodbye remembering she had thought about the possibilities and contingencies of an unruly client. Airlines experienced it, schools too, often ending in deaths, sad to say. The coffee shop next door had experienced it, causing Leroy, its owner unceremoniously to announce that he had taken the required course and now had a license to carry. And he did so visibly—his holstered M&P 9mm semi-automatic clearly at his side every time he reached up to roast beans or make a cappuccino or latte.

She had discussed the vetting and admission process for gym membership with her husband, although not yet extending it to the massage component. It struck her again that the fitness business was destined to attract a certain percentage of a violent, perhaps mentally disturbed clientele.

Just about anyone could join and sign up for a fitness or fight lesson. A high percentage of soldiers, maybe some with PTS were in law enforcement and a small number, but seldom identified, abusive individuals were attracted to police work. She'd bring up the whole issue again in a calmer moment with her husband and propose the need for a revised application for membership and admission.

It was dusk now and she helped sanitize the weights, checked all lights and the restrooms, let O'Toole and Foley out the door and locked it, reassuring them that she was fine and was headed straight home. She hoped Anthony was already there. She missed seeing the boys and having them sitting down for dinner. They were in college now at the University of New Mexico and lived in the Freshman dormitory, always busy with friends and they said, "studying." Nina decided to call home and yes, Tony was there but asked her to pick up some dinner at the Thai Kitchen: "Number forty-four, remember, Sweetheart, Sweet and Sour Shrimp, brown rice, add cashews and sticky fried rice with mango for desert. The usual, my Dear." She tried to laugh and said "Of course," telling him to expect her home around 6:30.

What she didn't expect, however, was the car tailgating her as soon as she turned off Second Street to Alameda Avenue. It was a tan, unmarked police car, with oodles of antennas, and with flashing lightbar lights. A siren blast made her flinch and right away she knew it was Aguilar, smiling like his gaping feline tattoo. He had followed her from the gym. He was clearly harassing her. She saw the outline of his laughing, squinty face and the red and blue lights reflecting on the lenses of his glasses. He had a bandaged nose and held a mic away from his mouth and his growling voice accosted her from the car's loud speaker, saying in a nasal tone, "Pull over, lady! You are obstructing traffic." But she wasn't.

Some cars had stopped at the intersection up ahead but there was no other car directly in front of her. She was scared! Her heart was pounding! So she slowed down and pulled into the mall parking lot. Aguilar didn't follow her, however, but sped off west on Alameda, gunning his car into the Hooters' parking lot, warning lights still blinking as if in a *Guillain-Barré*, spasmodic, code-three pursuit.

Nina grasped the steering wheel and sobbed in anger. Those poor girls are asking for it with that bastard!" she said. "That Goddamned bastard!" Her churning gut told her this was only the beginning. He was trouble and he was bringing it to her. She picked up the order at the restaurant and by the time she made it home, she'd almost had two wrecks, terrified that a police car would show up again and that Aguilar knew about her phone call to Captain Cain, and had radioed his police pals to arrest her.

Dinner was tense and she didn't eat anything much, telling her husband only that she's had a rough afternoon, one client after another, and that she was exhausted, had the beginnings of a migraine, and wanted to go to bed and sleep forever. The smell of the Thai food was making her nauseated and the house lamps were torture to her sensibility and finally in the bedroom she threw off her clothes, ridding herself of her tight, bothersome bra, only removed one sock, put her pajamas on wrong side out, not giving a damn about it, took an extra-strength Excedrin and replayed the pain-induced massage, egged on by the phantasmagoric mouse-devouring cat tattoo, wishing she had really hurt him, wanting another chance to pound the shit out of another miscreant now come into her life, again purely by chance. She thought all those hard emotional and violent times were behind her. Putting a cold wash-cloth compress on her head, she fought her way to a wakeful sleep with random images of her one-time 4-H goat. *Cabrón!*

In her dream a terrible weight was upon her, a large flat flagstone, the kind she had seen every day on the way to work stacked and for sale at the Stone Emporium on the corner of Montaño and Edith. A large forklift was picking up the flagstones and traveling sluggishly over to place them, one after another, on her body. The weight was enormous and she could feel her intestines being squashed, some starting to push out through her vagina and rectum. But then she noticed the visage of the forklift driver. It as Aguilar, dressed in his police uniform, and wearing huge slanted, cat-eye safety goggles and a leather hat made out of dead mice, mimicking a deranged Kamikaze pilot in WWII. And he was manipulating the machine so that the thick sharpened forks were like giant cat claws playing with her, scratching at her, trying to probe inside her and flipping her over on her stomach. Then the machine took on full feline form and it was Aguilar's animated tattoo come to life, and the weight was its ink and she was in its gaping mouth and it was on top of her and inside her too and she couldn't escape and she felt a claw transform into goat horns gouging through her stomach, her breasts and chest, tearing through her heart into her throat and neck and straight out the top of her eye-bulging head, pinning her to the bedroom wall.

Her agonizing scream roused her husband who came bursting into the room to hold and comfort her. "Rest easy Nina. *Calmaté.* Nothing to fear," he said, stroking her sweaty hair and head. "Just a nightmare. Try to go back to sleep. *Soy aqui a su lado.* I'm here. I'm here. We have Neighborhood Watch remember?"

And after she told him she had called the police on Aguilar and that she was deeply worried, they fell asleep in each other's arms. Outside, a patrol car cruised slowly by, its nervous cat-eye spotlight searching for house addresses.

4
LOS TEJANOS

Raul's conversation with Roscoe had been short. "Yes, there's a jaguar migrating up from Mexico. Reports have said he was black, panther like; others have said he's just a mountain lion with some kind of strange spots than shine like a mallard's feathers, iridescent in the dark; white-belly bright in the night; one report said it might be an offspring of *La Chupacabra* and has the ability to jump fifty feet horizontally or vertically; plus he can shape-shift and emit a camouflaging mist from its nostrils! I say "he" or "it" but we don't really know gender or how to classify it. We set up trail cameras and confirmed only that it's a cat, a big one. Male or female we don't know. We've put an endangered, protected species designation on him for now. No hunting! No bounties! So you be wary when those Tejanos come for you to guide them to the bears—I mean the beers! Encourage them to kill coyotes instead."

Roscoe had always been a sarcastic SOB and understandably didn't like the extra work caused by *Tejanos* and the reckless, littered footprint they left on the environment, be it campsite or trail. He understood the state's pampering them and the official encouragement to cut them some slack because of the economic boon provided by their tourism and licensing. It was mostly their damn egotism which pissed him off, and the exaggerated, nasal "Y'all" way they talked.

Raul didn't much care for their domineering personalities but he too appreciated and needed their money. Moreover, the approaching hunting season was complicated by this mysterious cat roaming the mountains and allegedly ranging down into the foot hills for a livestock kill, cattle or sheep—as well as a coyote-killing contest offering an assault rifle for a prize. Mix alcohol with gun powder and Texan braggadocio complete with their tall-tale tendencies and that spelled trouble. With just a few weeks before opening season and the first hunters due to arrive before that, Raul knew some overdue preliminary preparations were in order. First to the gun shop sponsoring the coyote kill and then a scouting trip to Manzano Peak and environs.

Smitty's Gun Shop didn't stock a large inventory—mostly shotguns and small arms guns like .22s. He did have deer hunting rifles, mostly .30-.30s, Winchester or Marlin, as well as a .300 Savage or two. He could and often did take special orders for more exotic rifles. This fall he had an M-16 displayed in the front window with a sign saying "First Prize! All you mangy coyotes better head for cover!" The ticket sales for entering the contest for a chance for the gun were brisk to say the least, with total sales numbering close to a hundred when Raul entered the store.

Jorge (Smitty) Sanchez left a scruffy customer to greet Raul at the handgun counter. *Hola compa, buscando para una pistola nueve, o grande, como Sucio* Harry, or just wanting to sign up for a chance at the assault rifle? Lots of coyote out your way. Bet you could win!"

Que dice, hermano? Raul replied and reached across the counter to shake hands. "Now Smitty, you know how I feel about these killing contests. Kill just to kill isn't the true hunter's way as we've discussed before, and you know it. Besides, *El Coyote* has its rights to make it if he can without facing a machine gun! No, I came in to remind you that the Tejanos will be here for their guided hunt, and to be sure you have enough ammo for them. Plus, I wanted to hear what you've heard about this reported jaguar roaming up this way. *Sabes tu?*"

"Lots of talk, Primo. Lots of talk. Some ranchers buying extra ammo if they think they've seen it. I guess it's possible. My grandfather used to talk about seeing a panther and hearing its blood curdling cries in the night. Grandfather said it was because the big cat couldn't find his home and was lost."

"I talked to Roscoe Powers, the old coot, and he says its real. They caught it on a trail camera and some department wardens found hairballs, scat, and tracks and Harley Shaw's dog Chink picked up its scent. They're happy about it. Encouraging it. But wary, like a cat, of the side issues too. Anyway, the Cat is back or his son or grandson maybe. But he's protected as endangered says Roscoe by national and state Game and Fish. Better advise the trigger-happy customers whoever they are that a coyote isn't a jaguar, but you know about itchy Tejano temptations."

~

It was no small matter for Raul to take off from his ranching duties with the livestock and the family. Estelle would miss him most, both for his company, and for his share of the work. His daughters were teenagers now and had all those accompanying worries and manic hopes and fears which needed a father. He always relied on his brother, Nina's father, Lalo, to shoulder most or the family and work load during his guided hunts. Tejanos were a pain in the ass but their money and *propinas grande* made up for the grief they caused. He'd convinced Lalo to make the short camping trip to Manzano Peak to size up the possibilities of a jaguar, of all places, in the Manzanos.

Lalo knew how to track better than anyone in that part of the state. He'd grown up there and gone to the mountains hundreds of times, all the way back to when he was a boy and took his first hunting trips there with his grandfather, before Raul was born. Lalo agreed to a weekend, finding all the talk about a jaguar enticing. He knew mountain lion tracks for sure and a jaguar's tracks couldn't be all that different.

Friday night before they were scheduled to leave and scout the place, Raul heard the phone ring. The area code of the call was 512. That area code, he recognized as in Texas. Round Rock to be exact. So he knew it had to be Bevin Ralston, the big-shot Shamrock oil and gasoline distributor who was bringing two of his corporate lacky friends, a Larry Grimes and a Herbert Wilson on the upcoming hunt. Raul walked into the kitchen to take the call, not without some reluctance if not trepidation—he'd wanted to check the mountain before any Texas talking. He grimaced to his wife when he picked up the phone and stretched out the curled cord to talk.

"How's *El Frijolito Saltón* today, Señor Raul?" Yes, confirmed. It was big shot Bevin, he was reluctant to acknowledge. But he gritted his teeth and said, "Pretty good, Bev—almost ready for the hunt. Going up there today with my brother to scout it out."

"That's what I'm calling about, *hermano. The Dallas Morning News* just ran an article, picked up from *The Santa Fe New Mexican* and *Albuquerque Journal* about Arizona and New Mexico wanting to reestablish the jaguar up there. Papers say there's been more than one sighting. Some trail cameras and trapping plans are underway and talk with a private zoo run by some Macho Camacho guy in Pagosa Springs, retired from trail guiding. You know about all that?

"Some rumors are mixed in there, I'm afraid. But yes there's talk about a jaguar in this vicinity. That's part of what I want to check on—to see if there is... and if it is anything for us to worry about. You'll have deer to shoot at and a foothills coyote-killing contest for manly-hearted men like you."

"Mean hearted? That's me. Like Jerry Lee, I'm a mother-humping killer! And WORRY about? Hell, I hope there is a Mexican jaguar on the run up there. If there is I'll shoot his greasy, beaner, spotted-ass and mount his stuffed, bowling-ball head and glass eyes in my office. I've got a big gun or two you know. I'll bring my Marlin .45-70 Big Bore. I once sent a moose into oblivion with it in Michigan."

"Oh no, Bevin! Not going to happen. Even if we were to see it we wouldn't condone shooting it. Protected you know. We'll let Game and Fish handle any ghostly jaguar. I'll know more about it after I go up to the mountains for a look."

"Oh hell yes, *Señor* Lucero. Who cares about a measly mule dee or a half-dozen coyote pelts? There's an extra thousand in it for you if you lead us to that spotted *chile con carne* devil out to kill us. We'll plead self-defense if we're caught. You think about that. See you in a week, Pussy Cat."

~

Raul and Lalo reminisced about their younger days in in mountains, as they drove east past Quarai to the Manzanos; and talked about their sheep and the drought and the hysteria developing about a possible jaguar coming down from the mountains to the farms and ranches. Raul asked about how Nina was doing in her new life and about how her brother, Rosendo, was doing in the big world of music. Raul finally mentioned the scream he'd heard a few weeks ago and summarized his talk with Roscoe and Bevin about jaguar sightings.

"Do you think we'll find any tracks, Lalo? They should look just like a lion's tracks, don't you think?

"About the same I would guess—maybe smaller. Granddad and dad mentioned seeing one, remember, although they talked about it as more of a spirit or ghost, a legend from days long past."

"Sometimes I think we are the ghosts, Lalo. And reality as we know it isn't real. *La vida no más que un sueño.*"

Too many "Twilight Zone" and "X-Files" reruns for you, my brother. But I know what you mean. It's just the perspective of growing old and feeling like your whole life is a dream. Like long ago was just yesterday. And I'm older than you! Just wait."

They reached the spot they knew so well, having set up camp there at the base of the peak on countless deer and turkey hunts. By the time the tent was up and a quick campfire made to heat up supper, darkness was upon them and they crawled into their bedrolls and zipped up the tent for the night. The owls kept them awake for only a short time before they were asleep with their respective jaguar dreams.

Raul was soon dreaming of the times he and Lalo went out with their father and the stories he told them under star-studded skies about the ruins. And he was talking to them again beside a dying campfire—how he'd heard about the ceremonies and blood sacrifices there and even found some remnant bones of animals including turkeys, deer, lions, and how he'd heard of an extra-large black panther who could throw off his spots like bullets and hypnotize his prey, be they cattle or people. People swore that during the day he was a barber with long black hair and blemished skin which some said was skin cancer. He could see the spots swirling in his dream and pictured Bruno Sisneros's ancestral face with its moles and warts and cheek scars, knowing deep down that the Sisneros ancestry of Shorty, his father's and his son's bloodline was one of misfits and some said brujos malditos from the underworld.

Word was he had even slit the throat of Pedrito Zamora and added his blood to the supply kept in cooling bottles in their storeroom refrigerator. Raul moaned in his sleep and remembered Shorty had nicked his ear last haircut. He'd had to keep it bandaged for days.

~

The next morning they had their strong coffee complete with grounds and some tasty over-cooked biscuits with honey out of their well-used Dutch oven which this time had been smothered in coals a bit too long. Then they went off in opposite directions taking stock of the condition of the drought-stressed landscape, bemoaning the lack of rain. The deer they both saw showed signs of the aridity and weren't as sleek and fat as they should be. But there were plenty in small herds and needed thinning out by the Texans who never really hunted for venison—just rack size.

Lalo was still munching on a dry biscuit when he saw the tracks. Cat tracks for sure, a bit blurred but fresh and no doubt, a cougar's prints. They led to a deer carcass—a young spike buck with its innards eaten out and teeth gouges on its throat. "The ways of Nature..." he mused, and then looked closer. There were claw marks on a nearby tree and tufts of hair sticking to some of the bark lower down. The hair was multi-colored, almost peacock like. If it had been a lion the hair would have been lighter in color. Scat too. No, this was evidence of another kind of predator. He pulled small bunches of the hair off the tree and stuck a wad of it in his pocket to show Raul. He finally found the camera application on his phone and took some upside-down pictures of the scat and paw prints, cursing beneath his breath about these blasted new-fangled contraptions.

~

Raul hadn't tracked far when he found a demolished trail camera. It was tipped over and torn more or less to pieces. He kicked the damaged tripod aside and picked up the main box and tried to get it running. He couldn't. He knew, however, that Roscoe would want to have it so stuffed it in his belt bag. While he was struggling with fitting it in and closing the zipper, he saw a flash of motion through the distant stand of juniper trees. It was fast but he was sure it was more than eye floaters. He walked softly in that direction, found some tracks and broken branches and confirmed he had seen an animal. The tracks were a combination of small tracks some becoming larger, then even larger then becoming wolf-like or coyote-like. As if a bobcat became an ocelot, soon became a mountain lion, then some kind of otherworldly, unclassified cryptid or hybrid creature out of folk lore or some children's book he had once seen matching different animal heads with different bodies.

Could a Chupacabra also be feline or have a cat-like counterpart, he wondered? Raul, hearing brush break, quickly looked up again to see only the rear splotchy, spotted haunches and tail of what had to be some sort of jaguar which soon crouched and sprung out of sight into its own deeply etched image. Raul had heard of the false science of cryptozoology. But now wondered if it was false! Had he experienced shape-shifting or metamorphosis first hand? Raul's grandfather, he remembered, had told of seeing some kind of spotted phantom cat one night near the ruin of Abo.

When Raul compared his experience with Lalo's and examined the tufts of retrieved hair and photographs his brother had taken…when Lalo heard about Raul's encounter, they were both more or less stupefied, wondering if any guided hunt with the Texans should be postponed or cancelled. No telling what they would see and do with some Jack Daniels and Coors under their belt and their big guns and fat, itchy fingers. On the other hand, maybe the much-rumored specter, the jaguar or phantom cat El Jefe, might eat them and eliminate the problem. Raul laughed to himself and made a mental note to inform Roscoe about the broken trail camera asking him to report on any confirming pictures.

5
SOY EL MIEDO

Felix Aguilar had grown accustomed, you could say addicted, to stopping off at Hooters between shifts, posting it as legitimate investigative work on his work log. And, in his mind, it was related to his ironic part in the investigation of the West Mesa murders—no one suspecting his true identity as the serial killer himself, creating or following one fraudulent or anonymous tip after another but in reality, investigating his criminal self, not his policeman self, looking to being promoted once he figured out how to claim the reward and who to really frame. He'd met his first victim there at Hooters, whatever her name was, and now he had his eye on another promising candidate: Lillian Gonzalez, a dark-skinned bosomy, vivacious, life-loving young Mexican girl from *Mazatlán*, just arrived in the city through the crossing at *Nogales*—a typical candidate with little money, few real friends or any local family.

He'd questioned her a couple of times, between ordering drinks, asked about her with her co-workers, and satisfied she was naïve enough to fall to the very end for his uniform, line of bull, and braggadocio. He just had to watch his temper. He half regretted his outburst of anger at the uncooperating massage therapist. He'd misjudged her, confusing a stereotypical masseuse's role with a true professional role. "It would still be loads of fun to do her in," he thought "when the right time and place presented itself."

This particular early fall evening a sand storm had kicked up over the West Mesa so that even the volcanoes couldn't be seen. Most people took them for granted and never even noticed the white painted "J' on the largest middle volcano. Saint Joseph's College was gone but their initial remained on the lava rocks. Felix, however, having little faith in the Chaste Saint, used it as a directional marker for the initial graves, more or less in plain sight. There was a severe storm and localized lightning warning broadcast over cell-phones, and Felix figured it would make for a good excuse to convince Lillian to let him take her home.

He entered Hooters on his way home and took his usual place at the corner of the bar so he could see the door and most of the tables. Everyone recognized him and took him for a good-looking Chicano who was a rising star in the department. They often razed him about the recent time he'd caught his Sam Brown belt pepper spray canister on the edge of the stool and they had to call the fire department to vacate the building. He made the best of their collective joking too. He did little without some alternative motive in mind. He still had to fight spontaneity—like his outburst with the tempting, fucking massage therapist. He'd once seen a Poe "Purloined Letter" movie in a class as part of his certification in criminal justice at the local Technical Vocational Institute and was now convinced that the best way to hide things was to place them out in the open. Or play the role of a klutz when in reality on top of it all.

He asked Masie, to him a floozy barmaid, about Lillian. "Oh, she's in the staff room in the back, changing clothes, having a cigarette, getting ready to go home...just waiting out the storm I guess."

"Tell her I can take her home. I'm off duty and need to do my friendly officer pay it forward good deed of the day."

"Sure you are. But I'll tell her. She's not too keen on waiting on busses in a sandstorm."

Before Felix had half-finished his *Dos Equis* lager,

Lillian was at his side, hovering close on the next stool, saying in broken English, "So, you to take me... home? *En la tormenta? Vamos a mi casa juntos, contigo en su auto policia?*"

He gave her a hug pulling lightly at her back-brassiere strap and led her out the door, pretending she was under arrest. The sand stung as it hit their faces and he let her open the passenger door herself. The wind blew her dress up over her waist revealing her rounded butt in her skin-tight leggings, causing her ersatz chauffeur, already seated and turning on the ignition, to rub his groin and catch his breath.

She got in the car, complaining of the sand stinging her legs. Nervously rubbing them for comfort, she was as excited as a school girl on career day, asking questions about the radio, the shotgun standing cold and hard between them but in easy reach of the driver, the siren and beacon lightbar switches.

"You live out on Ninety-eighth right? Or is it Unser?

"*Si, Calle Ninety-eighth.*"

"You ever see the volcanoes up close, *amor?* The lava rocks and the petroglyphs? It's a lousy day with all the sand but that will make them seem more other worldly."

"*Los vulcanes? Sí, sí, vamos a ver.*"

So Felix took the long way to her home, planning that this circuitous route would become somewhat familiar to her on her destined last ride some moonlit night in the future. The sandstorm beat tiny pits in the car's glass and paint, having its way against the windshield and the doors, telling him to wait. Wait for a more compliant time. He stepped on the accelerator, flicked the switch for the beacon light, turned to her, and said, "Later baby, *Hoy en dia los volcanes son deprimentes. Vamos a su casa ahora, Lillian.*"

Since her attempted assault by the monstrous cat-tattooed Aguilar, Nina had been afraid of her own shadow, yet resolved to workout even harder and take on the Everlast heavy bag with new strength and determination. She'd also gone to Calibers gun shop and bought a .380 S&W, M&P automatic as well as seeking Leroy's advice and signing up for a concealed carry permit. A little practice added to the bill and she was soon a decent shot.

The gun became a close companion, a friend she named "Jackson" after the deadly jacketed hollow-point bullets Raul recommended she use. She and Jackson shopped together and Nina tried to calm herself and erase the egregious mouse-eating cat tattoo from her memory and mind. When she practiced shooting she shot at homemade cat targets, always aiming for the mouth, imagining blowing the poor inked mouse into oblivion with the cat's head.

Thursday was the day she went shopping to Costco for groceries and supplies and this particular Thursday was a kind of turning point, causing her to go to a counsellor for help with her phobia. The lot was busy and frantic as usual, with hardly any parking spots—so people were stressed out and tense as they went from lane to lane looking for a place to park.

When a big Tundra took a spot she intended to use, she reached for her gun. She took it out of the seat console and was ready to roll down the window and wave it at the big red-neck driver until she got better control of herself, saying, "Jesus Christ! What's wrong with me? I could kill that bastard. I do need help!" So she backed off and found another parking spot where she sat and sobbed for a good ten minutes.

Her fears continued, however, and even increased. She moved her pistol to her side for easier access and removed the hammer strap for a faster draw—a move she practiced in front of a mirror at home. Her nightmares grew more grotesque and she started hoping a stray cat would jump out in front of her car so she could run over it.

Her therapist diagnosed her as having a "Zoo

phobia," began some cognitive behavioral exercises, and advised her, ironically, to get a cat, preferably a kitten, and nurture it to see if, in a kind of homeopathic way exposure to her fear might lessen it. "That's damn counter intuitive," she thought but resolved to follow the suggestion when she got time.

One day at Smith's grocery store she was browsing the wine selections and an elderly man in ragged clothes, and uncombed hair, his face red from sun or from a serious rosacea complexion, reached in front of her and quickly grabbed a bottle of *Saint Clair pinot noir*, rammed it under his coat and started running down the aisle, heading out of the store. Nina started yelling, "*Ladrónes dentro la tienda!* Thief! Thief!" and drew her pistol, pointing it up in the air and began shooting wildly at a "Most Interesting Man" beer poster—emptying the clip!

Amidst all of the customer commotion the manager and a couple of stock boys caught the old man at the door. He went into a cursing rage calling for someone to "stop that crazy murdering bitch." All of the questions when the police arrived were directed to Nina. Did she have a license to carry? Had the man assaulted her? Did she think stealing a bottle of wine deserved that reaction? Had she taken the time to really evaluate the situation? She was let go and sent on her way to continue shopping. Although all the customers had been frightened, ducking for cover, it was Nina who was most frightened—scared of herself.

Her massage therapy appointments had all but stopped. She still gave Anthony his weekly massage and minimally kept up the laundry and the massage room for him. But her gym time was all the grind of kettlebells as she progressed from heavier to heavier weights becoming more discerning with her growing proficiency, training now almost exclusively with "Kettlebell Kings" brand—even seeking out an endorsement deal when going to Denver for certification. Finally she realized she was getting a bit ahead of herself in such ambition and settling into daily workouts via video programs and tapes. Her strength and technique grew session by session and she knew, all things considered, she could beat the crap out of any man who accosted her or even looked cross-eyed at her.

Her shopping trips became rituals of staring down people who wouldn't move their carts or who lingered to stare at her now rippling muscles and impressive physique. One poor stock boy happened to look up at her from his kneeling position and she knocked off a row of canned peas on his head. Her still boiling anger and urge for revenge simmered deep inside her, growing proportionately with her strength and confidence. She decided to find Aguilar and investigate him and his habits on and off duty. She was convinced not only that he was a bad person but a corrupt cop. She set about to ruin his career and mess with his mind the way he had hers. "Don't stalk a stalker" became a repeated mantra for her. She remembered his turning into Hooters that first night and she soon staked out the place and, over a drink or a light meal, began asking questions of some of the waitresses, some of whom became leery of her intentions as solicitations.

One young voluptuous beauty named Lillian Gonzales told her one afternoon that she knew the man she was asking about, saying he had taken her home during a sand storm and was very polite. Conversations with others about past staff who subsequent to their association with him had disappeared. Nina knew she now had the nails for the bastard's coffin. The sooner she got the hammer, the better for *pobricita* Gonzales. "That Internal Affairs woman had better ratchet up her investigation," she sighed into her drink.

Nina worried constantly about Aguilar finding out about her call and her snooping—or walking into the place and seeing her. Even with that worry, however, her resolve and suspicions grew stronger, confirming the need to bring down this *pendejo* policeman.

6
VIVIR O MORIR

Ralston and his *lambe* cohorts from his company made an egregious grand entry to the little town before driving out to meet Raul at the ranch. They drove a GMC Denali SUV coated with highway grime and country road dust and mud splashes. Their white, black-lettered Texas plates were so covered with mud they were illegible. Even the lone star looked like a glob of caliche mud. They had littered their way up from El Paso and Las Cruces with empty beer bottles and Jim Beam whisky miniatures. The obsequious Mountainair constable Calvin Woods followed at a distance but held back due to the understanding that they brought in needed income to the small town. Their horns worked with plentiful ringing, supplemented by a recording of a castrated steer, bawling from a customized, thousand-dollar, fender-mounted horn. Even the cattle in the adjacent fields cringed at such sophomoric foolishness.

Raul was even more shocked this trip by the arsenal they brought with them. Ralston had his Big Bore Marlin uncased, hoping to maybe get a shot from the highway. His companions had the fanciest hand-carved leather cases for their guns Raul had ever seen, with *Mannlicher-Schönauer* labeling. When he commented on the name, Larry spoke up and said, "Hemingway's favorite gun, my man. Quite famous."

After introductions and a quick respite and snack prepared by Raul's wife, Estelle, they loaded their equipment into Raul's pickup and the skinny guy commented on the trailer carrying an ATV: "Who gets to ride in the dune buggy boss?"

"For carrying the game you're gonna shoot," Raul replied, "Much easier with it."

"I want to drive it," Larry chimed in, "Just like my customized golf cart back home."

Ralston said, "You'll wind up with a DUI for sure if any game wardens are around. You crashed into a tree at the country club last I remember."

Raul did his best to hide his derision at these three rich stooges he hypocritically tolerated only for their money. And that compromise promised to wear thin this trip what with his worries about the phantom jaguar.

They made it to the campsite and set up the tent, the Coleman stove, made a small piñon fire, set out the array of folding camp chairs and settled back for their respective habitual beverages. Raul went over the rules for the hunt stressing to refrain from shooting if they occasioned the possibility of seeing a jaguar. He would lead them out early in the morning, stressing the importance of gun safety and positioning so as not to shoot in each other's direction.

"Carry your guns with safeties on and watch me for my hand signals when to shoot and when not to shoot. No lions! No bears!" clearing his throat he emphasized, "No jaguars!" Explaining again that this hunt's licenses and tags were for deer. And only bucks. "No does." Ralston scoffed audibly and Larry and Herbert seemed impatient with all the rules, fearful and fidgety at the mention of maybe getting shot or shooting each other.

They rose before sunrise, dressed in their expensive Orvis boots and camouflage gear (and unbeknownst to Raul their canteens heavy with vodka) had their coffee, eggs, bacon, and tortillas prepared hot and ready by Raul, begrudging having to wait on such helpless, dislikable fellows. The thought of their money again assuaged his unease.

Raul knew the trails, canyons, and hills he wanted to hit and in what order.

He'd always found a herd of deer in a special canyon half way up Manzano peak where juniper started to be replaced by ponderosa pines and the land levelled out into a table-top mesa. He hoped for them to reach it before noon.

The complaints started about an hour into the hike. "What the hell, man, where are the fucking deer?" Ralston whined. "We've haven't seen anything but a lousy tassel-eared squirrel and dried shit pellets!" "Yeah, my damn gun is getting heavy. It ain't got no hand-carved leather strap like Larry's," Herbert grouched. "Shut your shitty complaining, Herbert," Larry grumbled. "Just like back at the office, always having to put up with you and your guff. Get a life Buster! Buy yourself a goddamn strap like I did."

Raul was about to tell them both the shut the hell up when he saw it.

He thought, at first, it might be another hunter because of the camouflaged patterns jumping through some lingering junipers. Raul's arm went up and his hand formed a fist shape. The trio of malcontents stopped, flipped off their safeties and raised their guns. Raul motioned them to spread out and pointed right and left of where they clustered. He continued slowly and quietly walking straight ahead, straining his eyes to see again what he had seen. Larry flared right, Herbert turned left, and Bevin stopped where he was, then started backing up and moving sideways, keeping his head cocked skyward and looking into the taller trees, certain he'd seen what Raul had seen, a conglomeration of dancing, blurred spots. Until...he tripped...and, as he was falling his gun went off. The Big Bore bullet went straight into Larry's side, blowing half his chest away. Herbert, hearing the shot, fired wildly in Raul's and Bevin's direction. His bullet hit Bevin, knocking him down to the ground, his ankle blasted to smithereens.

Herbert and Bevin were screaming and cursing, asking for help. Raul kept calm, trying to get hold of himself and apply basic first aid until he could come back with the ATV.

"But what about the jaguar?" Bevin asked, nearly delirious. I saw the damn thing. I saw it."

"So did I," "So did I," Raul kept repeating, as he ran, stumbling, back to get the ATV.

El Jefe, now deeper into the brush, paid them all little mind, remembering times long past when Hernán Cortés and his lieutenants had tried to capture him. Qué tonto! Fools all! Except for the Nahua woman La Malinche. For her, as a compatriot, he had empathy. La Llorona! Together they roared, cried, and commiserated.

As soon as Roscoe Powers heard about the accident and needing to check on the Game and Fish camera he drove down to Mountainair to get the story from Raul and Demetrio Gurlé, the Torrance county coroner. Roscoe met Raul at the Rite Spot Diner next to Shorty's Barbershop. Roscoe was a flamboyant fellow, albeit something of a grouch. They said he'd arrest his own brother if he found him over the limit, past shooting times, or without a license. Word was he had even invented some laws on the spot. In a word, most people were a little afraid of Roscoe. He wore his sidearm high on his waist and preferred an Army issue 1911 Colt Government .45 to a Beretta or a Glock. He'd had an extra spotlight installed on his patrol car and drove an old Ford Victoria police interceptor which he kept well-tuned with the best safety Goodyear tires.

Raul was waiting in a booth when Roscoe came through the door. Some of the barbershop customers were at the counter flirting with Irene Metzger (a full-figured woman with a special wiggle in her walk) gabbing about the shooting, and wanting to talk to Raul too. Manny Sisneros was standing at the side of the booth with one arm stretched across the vinyl back, trying to touch Raul's hair. Raul tried to shoo him away but laughingly promised to get a manicure once hunting season was over. "You promise, Mr. Raul! You better damn well promise," Manny said as he lingered and brushed shoulders with Roscoe as he was scooting into Raul's booth.

"Take a load off, Roscoe. What' your pleasure?" Raul said and motioned across the room to Irene, and continued, risking kidding the big man, saying, "You think you can fit that big gun and belly in here?"

"Coffee and a bear claw, will do me." He said with more chagrin than grin.

"Do you want to know what was on the camera or not? We developed what you retrieved and you remember meeting Lowell Smith, our magazine photographer when he came up here some time back, found the camera where you said he would, and saved some film from another camera you had missed. And both places, biggest damn cat any of us have ever seen.

Bigger than a lion but shouldn't ought to be. Jaguar hybrid of some kind. Plenty of spots like a leopard but much larger than your ordinary jaguar. So, we want it to live and we hope trap it for Ray's Rocky Mountain Museum. Tell your damn Texans not to fire even one bullet at it. Not one! This is historic, ecological, biological stuff. And we can maybe use this prowler cat to help establish them back here in New Mexico again. There are sightings over in Arizona too and some anticipated trapping. Who knows, we may find it to be a lover once we determine its gender."

"*Jesus de Cristo*, Roscoe. Right here in my nearby mountains! We all had suspicions—sounds, stories, rumors running rampant. Now we have proof."

This was exciting news to Manny too when he overheard Roscoe's news.

And he began telling everyone in the café about it as he headed back to the barbershop to tell Shorty. "A jaguar in town! A jaguar in town! My, my, my goodness! I'm getting a gun, a big, fast-shooting one," he could be heard saying as he exited the café. "Kill the damn coyotes but catch the beautiful jaguar."

"But Raul, tell me a bit more first-hand information about the shooting accident of the Texan? Are you sure it was an accident? Coroner's report says he was pretty much blown to bits by his boss's gun. What a cannon! I only saw a photograph. That was ugly enough for me."

"*Que lastima*! Yes, pretty sure it was an accident. Camouflage mistaken for a jaguar's spots, it was. He stumbled and fell with the safety off, trying to get a shot at the phantom jaguar. The two employees carped a bit about work and their guns; however, nothing more, unless there's some other corporate or office history I don't know anything about," said Raul. "Boss shoots employee! Brings new meaning to being 'fired,' right?"

"That's a pretty crude thing to say, Raul, but you always did have a talent for saying too much or too little or for just...too, too. Straight talker though. No filter is okay sometimes. As for the coyote shoot, I'll be checking limits on that. I'll be coming in and out of town for a time this fall.

Raul picked up the check, paid pretty Irene, and said good bye to Roscoe as he scooted, hemmed and hawed, into his archaic Crown Vic. "These Texans are the least of my problems now, Raul thought. A jaguar in my mountains. *Nuestro abuelo Don Hilario* must be rolling over in his grave with Beethoven and Tchaikovsky," he chuckled.

7
COMPENSACIÓN

Felix didn't give up his dastardly plans for Lillian. She was too ripe and too tempting. He had to be extra special going back to the same well for water, so to speak. The last victim had been a Hooters' waitress, and from Mexico too—extra young, extra naïve, and she had put up a struggle there at the end. He planted her several hundred yards from the others, closer to the petroglyphs, and now that his investigation officers were using not only dogs but United Rentals' Bobcats, another body had been found.

Lillian would make two—maybe three, he'd forgotten numbers and their full names—all waitresses, or dancers, or to him prostitutes, thinking El Norte would be the promised land but finding a serial killer, a devil disguised as the law, *La Ley*, *la policia* more deranged and more dangerous than the corrupted *Federales* back home. Fragile, gentle, feminine hopes literally turned to the dust of Albuquerque's desolate West side, the badlands symbolized by lava beds and mesas populated by a landfill and a city prison, the city's human and industrial trash, and now the shifting-sand graves of ill-fated women and thousands of greedy, consumer ravaged people's garbage dumped in arroyos and trenches reaching beyond the purple-gold clouds and orange sunsets of the western horizon.

Lillian's compensation for her northern pilgrimage was soon to be bestowed in the form of suffocation. Felix, once knowing where she lived, had asked her out for a take-out meal from Mac's La Sierra Steak house and a picnic along the Rio Puerco, driving back to Nine Mile Hill to look at the city lights. She thought she was in heaven there beside this handsome and humorous manly man, and unbeknownst to her she was soon to be there.

Felix knew it wasn't wise to drive his own car this night—his well-kept and commodious black 300 Chrysler sedan with tinted windows and a tiny pin-striped cat on the trunk lid. He spoke Spanish which she appreciated but thought it strange in his pronunciations and vocabulary, more riddled with Spanglish than she preferred. She thought, however, this is the Spanish of the north, her new home and she tried hard to retain the unfamiliar words, even asking for Felix to repeat himself if she was dumbfounded at what he was saying. There was no misunderstanding of his actions though. He gave her some pills saying they were harmless but enhanced a blissful feeling, words she thought sounded like kissing. He was not just rough but merciless in his lovemaking, forcing her into contorted car-seat positions and to her unknown acts outside on the hood and trunk during sex. He told her she had to climax at the very moment he would release his hands from her throat. She then couldn't breathe and at the most intense moment she lost consciousness. She was still alive though. He was satisfied beyond his expectation and said, actually purred the words "*A la major, a la major, la dia de paga puta estupida*, and that's where you soon will be—underground in this god-forsaken *tierra mala.*"

Felix paid little attention to the initials and brief inscriptions, the crude faces and distorted animals etched in the lava rocks—at least he never had before. This time however, with each shovel-full of sand tossed on Lillian's lifeless body one particular animal figure seemed to glare down at him in the moonlight, "*Ojo malo...huye*, get away," Felix kept repeating, as if some dirt dauber or pesky horse fly kept loitering over his head. The glaring eyes directed at him from an overhanging lava rock like a laser were those of a primitive yet easily recognizable cat with stippled white spots covering its entire body. He identified it as a leopard or a panther, at once curiously ancient and modern.

At one point he thought he saw Lillian move and raise her hand to him. He could feel the ground trembling, or was it his own hands losing his grip on the shovel. He jerked out of the way, raised his shovel ready to swing it, convinced that the figure on the rock was springing out at him or that the rock itself was shifting, trembling, and wavering—ready to fall! Was Lillian trying to pull him into her grave, he shuddered to think!

He soon resumed shoveling, however, and attributed his fears to imagined volcanic tremors and hallucinations caused by taking too many of the pills he habitually used in his string of murderous seductions.

~

Nina's therapy was in a later phase. Her anger was subsiding. Her skittishness was too. Her strength was growing. She had locked-in her planned strategy for revenge. Her relationship with Anthony and his tender loving ways had restored her own enjoyment of love making. Now and then the grinning, threatening face of her egregious one-time client and his grotesque cat tattoo would flash before her mind. Dr. Rafael (Rafa) Gomez, her therapist at UNM Medical had worked hard trying to make her face rather than run away from or bury her fear and anger. She thought him a nerdy fellow with his Z-coil shoes and his tattered green scrubs, but she followed his advice—up to a point. The suggestion of target practicing and carrying a pistol hadn't worked out exactly as planned. But that had helped make her feel more secure. Now she carried mace, intended for dogs. He had earlier also encouraged getting a kitten and devising games for them to play together. "A cat will demonstrate independence," he assured her, "but will also revive your mothering instincts with its purring and kneading. Nothing quite like having your cat play with a whimsical toy or brush up against your leg—you'll see Nina."

"Shit on a stick, Nina, said. What's to lose. I'll try it to shut up, if nothing else, to shut up the darn doc." So Nina grudgingly went to the city Animal Rescue Center and got a kitten. It was a Tabby cat with white stripped cheeks and all the distinctive patterns of that particular coat. She almost named it "Camella" but decided on "Carmella" because of its yellow caramel coloring.

Nina had some interesting times with her little cat, a little cat which soon grew into a big cat. She was amazed and totally impressed by Carmella's athleticism and the distances it could jump, both horizontally and vertically. It bore no resemblance the cartoonish Felix the Cat. And yet it was a cat and had a mind of its own which frustrated Nina and one night she grew so overwrought with its trying to climb up the curtains or hide under the bed—and having constantly to change the cat litter, that one night she thought of drowning it in the bathtub! When she cooled off a bit she put "You Damn Cat" outside and left it there until around 10:30. When she opened the door to look for Carmella, and feeling remorse for her heartless action, there wasn't a cat to be found.

She convinced Anthony to help her look around the neighborhood. He did, but with no results. The next morning they looked again. Still no Carmella.

"To hell with that," Nina thought. "Cats roam and take up with other people, other houses. Truth be told I don't like any kind of cat—real or in ink. Never did. Never will."

Once at the gym, she asked Anthony to help her work out with mitts that morning. "I need to get rid of my frustrations, sweetheart. Let's hit a bit!" She was unusually aggressive he felt right away, once they got going: swinging wildly, hitting hard, grimacing and moaning with each rapid hit. Anthony stopped, held the mitts to the side and said to his wife, "Take it easy, Nina, you're gonna blow out your wrists and knock me off balance. Maybe switch to the heavy bag and hit that for a while. What's the matter? The stupid cat isn't worth all this care and stress."

Not only did she shift to pounding the heavy bag, she went to the TRX straps and did countless squats one after the other, without rest. Then she picked up two twenty-five-pound steel plates and farmer walked them until she staggered and collapsed, saying "Damn it to hell! I've had it. I've fucking had it with all these healthy, physical and mental health remedies for that *pendejo* cop's harassment. I'm heading back home for a refreshing soak in the tub and a chilled bottle of Decoy rosé! Then to bed to sleep for a week! He and everybody else who fucks with me can go to hell—*chingada*!"

8
La Noche de Fuego

El Jefe had been bothered lately by dreams and ancient memories somehow coded in his blood and nerves. He had no use for the fat Texans and their proclivity to shoot each other rather than him. But he had felt Malinche was calling to him and he envisioned her avatar being buried amidst a field of petroglyphs, one in particular with his visage chiseled on it suspended over her body. He remembered the ancient times of the volcanoes where such large lava rocks had tumbled out of the earth, eventually cooling. And he saw the many people coming to draw him and others of his kingdom on the rocks. And he remembered this one representation of him with fire coming out of his mouth and his body stippled with ash over his inflamed orange-colored coat burning bright. And he rose and shook his powerful body, opening his mouth with a tremendous roar, loud enough to shake and rumble again the long-extinct volcanoes throughout Lavaland.

To the West and North on the bad-lands mesa near Albuquerque, Felix Aguilar first felt the ground shake when he fired up his Zippo for a smoke, then at a glance registered what he thought was a smile on Lillian's partially buried face—just before he was crushed by the teetering huge rock with an ageless, primitive cat etched on it!

Aguilar was done for, the cat caught instead of the mouse, like the rotten rodent rat he was. His just-lit cigarette dropped to the ground with him. Both legs were crushed and he lay on his back parallel to ill-fated Lillian. His anguished eyes stared across the black fields of lava rocks. The smiling full moon seemed intent on extending his pain and he at first yelled out for help then reconciled himself to first talking, then whispering, and finally mumbling to his dead conquest, looking trance-like at his red glowing cigarette as he reached out to touch her sorrowful face.

No human heard him *in extremis* and the distant glowing neon and twinkling colorful lights of the city, the green light atop the mountain tram station, and the Cibola Café on Sandia crest were oblivious to all—except for the merriment and conversation of lovers ordering one more last-call romantic drink before heading back down on the final tram ride of the night to their cars, quiet and cold in the parking lot.

Had they dared to look or been able to see that far, not only the rice grass, but the dried tumbleweeds were beginning to smolder and flame up, lending a diabolical glow to the two still, side by side, seemingly embracing bodies.

~

Nina and Tony awakened to coffee and toast and the shocking television news that the West Side killer had been caught and that he was, of all things, the very detective who was investigating the heinous case. Nina choked on her coffee and burned the toast when she heard Betty Ortiz, morning hostess on KOB's "Rise and Shine" show, look bleary-eyed into the cameras in a closeup revealing her hurried and partially smeared Breaking-News makeup say:

"Albuquerque people, this is shocking news! The West Mesa murders have apparently been solved! State Police and local FBI just announced that early this morning park rangers, answering calls about a brush fire and frantic calls about rumbling

volcanoes erupting and a possible minor earthquake, discovered two bodies, one in an open grave and one lying next to it with shovel at hand. The woman is identified as twenty-six-year-old Lillian Gonzales, recently relocated here from Mexico. The male body was identified as APD crime scene investigator, sergeant Felix Aguilar, incredulously her apparent killer.

Speculation is that he must have been uncovering the grave of Ms. Gonzales as part of his investigation. But evidence at the scene reveals he and he alone was the egregious grave digger and alleged murderer of not only the Gonzales woman but two other women also previously found buried on the mesa in graves only a few hundred yards from this most recent victim. Moreover, he had just recently been under Internal Affairs investigation for a reported attack on another woman.

The regional office of the State Police and Captain Will Bradford assume charge of the continuing investigation with the assistance of FBI agent Red Anderson stationed here. The Governor released a statement pledging full state resources in support of the request by Mayor Celso Davis to take the investigation out of the hands of municipal law enforcement because of 'conflicts of interest,' given the involvement and alleged culpability of a member of the city's own police department."

Nina was utterly speechless at the news but spurted out, "Damn it, Tony! He's the one! He's the bastard I told you about! Oh, Tony! the one who accosted and threatened me at the Gym!"

"My God, Nina, you're so damn lucky! We're so damn lucky!" Tony exclaimed. "It could have been you dead out there!"

Aftershock upon aftershock, as Nina tried to compose herself, pouring a glass of wine, the telephone rang. Nina sensed it was more alarming news about Aquilar and his victims; however, when Tony answered the phone it was her father, Lalo, calling.

"Sure Lalo, Tony said. She's right here."

When she took the receiver, she could tell by his quivering voice that her father was shaken.

"Nina, dear one, he said, I have bad news. Your mother was hospitalized last night. Can you come home to be with her?"

"What! Oh, God, no!" she moaned. Linda, Linda's in the hospital. Why? What's the matter with her?"

"She's been having pains and overall internal discomfort. The doctor here says it's cancer but she'll need more tests in Albuquerque, at the Anderson Center there. Can you help us through that?"

"Of course...sure thing, Dad. I'm on my way home today. I should be there by nightfall. Are Raul and Estelle there? Have you phoned Rosendo?"

"Yes, they're here and I reached Rosendo in Los Angeles. He'll arrive first thing tonight."

"What is it Nina?" Tony asked. Your mom?"

"Cancer!"

9

ELLA VUELVE

El Jefe continued coming along, feeling relieved that his purpose was being fulfilled. He had reestablished himself back in his homeland of Aztlán, and felt its presence bone and soul deep. He had remedied what needed remedying in homage to Malinche. And he had found a willing partner high in the top tiers of Manzano Peak, a mountain lioness who recognized her destiny to merge with his, El Jefe, the immortal cat known first to the *Ancianos del sur.*

She would bring forth a new combined species of jaguar and mountain lion who would continue to be a beacon, a match for all seeking to keep the light of legend alive. El Jefe knew he was home. He was in and of this place. He would not die. He would continue coming along being himself and the hero of his own legend and occasion.

Raul was at peace knowing the jaguar he was sure he had seen was real and protected from the boorish Tejanos. He had chased a pickup full of coyote hunters off his land, explaining to them he and his land had no patience for such contests and if a coyote wandered onto his land he would take care of it.

In the meantime, Carlos Muñoz had bagged three of the poor varmints and claimed the M-16 prize at the gun shop, arranging to display his processed, tanned and mounted victims as "shaggy" wall hangings in Shorty's barbershop.

Nina headed south preparing for the ordeal she faced. She knew it would be one of toughest things she'd ever face.

EPILOGUE

I've learned many things through the ages. Yes, I'm an animal, a jaguar, "El Jefe," as it happens in the nominal known. But so are you. An animal. You can't deny it. You are animals!

I may not be human and may speak a different language, make different sounds, gutturals, labials and such as Wallace Stevens says, but narrative relates us, combines us, *conjunto*. For me and for you it's all one big story. We are born. We live. We die. "Variations on a motif," as they say.

For children, their parents grow old. For parents, their children never really grow up. The bond is eternal like the old adage says, somewhere in the aging process adults become children—"once a man twice a child."

Or as that 2,500 year-old, cat-like Sphinx asks, "What walks on four legs in the morning, two legs at noon, and three legs in the evening?" No cane needed by me thank the gods. Meow! Grrrrrr!

Parents eventually rely reciprocally on their children. There's no stronger bond, love, or loyalty like that of a mother for her child.

There's no more ferocious animal than a mother defending her offspring.

It's true throughout the animal kingdom and among humans that same inheritance holds. And a father? He protects spouse and offspring.

Family is the basis of continuance. *La familia* is what gives us strength to meet life's vicissitudes and sorrows. The will to tell our stories about how we get through with a little help, animal to animal, human to human.

So far...we endure. Prevail? Well, that's another story. What do you say we get on with it and keep on coming along?

The End...for now

READERS GUIDE

Chapter 1: *La Noche*

1. Translate the title.
2. Why is Spanish more appropriate than, say, French?
3. Who or what is "El Jefe"—man, god, beast, myth?
4. Is it credible for an animal to speak to the reader?
5. What is poetic license and how does it apply here?
6. Are you willing to suspend your disbelief?
7. Does this seem to be a fable? An allegory?
8. What is Magical Realism and which authors are known for it?

Chapter 2: *La Pelaqueria*

1. Why is a barbershop appropriate opening scene?
2. Are the people portrayed characters or caricatures? Why?
3. What seems to be the intended theme?
4. Is Manuel Sisneros likable or unlikable?

5. Is he more or less sympathetic than his father?
6. Do you find any humor in character portrayals and actions?
7. Would you have your hair cut at The Razor's Den?
8. Is Manny a reliable manicurist?
9. Why is he so friendly with Raul?
10. Is Raul at all similar to the Marlborough Man?
11. Are gender roles portrayed as macho and effeminate offensive to you?
12. Do you sense town fear or apprehension about a phantom jaguar?
13. Where is Elephant Butte in relation to Mountainair?
13. Do you anticipate Roscoe Powers to be a main character?

Chapter 3: *Manos de Oro*

1. What stereotypes apply to massage therapists?
2. What qualifies as a true professional masseuse?
3. Is strength a prerequisite?
4. Is Nina new in her role as a massage therapist?
5. What is her main character trait, her main ability?
6. Is Felix Aguilar's name intended as having figurative language applications?
7. Have you seen a Felix the Cat cartoon or drawing?
8. Is Nina in effect asking for it? Is that a fair question?
9. Is the sexual language offensive? Too cute? Fitting?

10. Does Felix deserve a broken nose? Is that too mild a punishment?

11. Is it convincing that a cop could be a sexual predator?

12. How are his name and stalking behavior intended to relate to El Jefe's?

13. Is the massage room located in the larger gym?

14. Would you hesitate to call the cops on a cop?

15. Is Nina's nightmare scary and effectively grotesque or over the top?

Chapter 4: *Tejanos*

1. Do you think New Mexicans resent Texans generally?

2. What traits does the stereotyped Texan display?

3. Would a Texan find this chapter entertaining? Repulsive?

4. Is Raul a dyed in the wool hypocrite? Is his hypocrisy understandable?

5. Is Bevin Ralston too much the buffoon?

6. Do Lalo and Raul confirm that a real jaguar exists in the mountains?

7. What is a cryptid and is it convincing that Raul knows about cryptozoology?

8. Is the plot close to reality? Are jaguars being reintroduced in the Southwest?

9. Why are animals given names beside their species or biological name?
10. Why is taxonomy such a good friend to biologists?

Chapter 5: *Soy El Miedo*

1. In what way is Albuquerque's West Mesa a forlorn and foreboding locale?
2. Why does Felix frequent establishments such as Hooters? Have you been there?
3. Any local history at work here in a convincing way?
4. What effect on events does the sandstorm have?
5. Are the volcanoes even close to being active? What's the intended dramatic effect?
6. Is Nina's post-traumatic stress credible? Laughable? An attempt at comic relief?
7. Is her decision to turn the tables and stalk Felix expected and welcome?
8. If Aguilar is such a detective why does he not foil Nina's inquiries?

Chapter 6: Vivir O Morir

1. When the ATV is first introduced do you anticipate its use as an expanding referent?
2. Do the brands and calibers of the guns really matter? How so?

3. Are Bevin and his lackies typical hunters?

4. How do you suppose the narrator and the author regard hunting? Hunters?

5. Are Larry and Herbert cast in the shadow, the tradition of Laurel and Hardy?

6. How does El Jefe regard the entourage?

7. What is your attitude toward zoos and wildlife museums?

8. Should Roscoe be dramatized as thinner and more heroic? Do you like him?

9. Is too much detail devoted to cars throughout?

10. Is Manny more macho than when first encountered?

11. Could Irene be written out of the story?

Chapter 7: *Compensación*

1. Are Aguilar's seductions convincing?

2. Would a serial killer drive his own car on such misadventures?

3. What mystical qualities can petroglyphs be conceived to have?

4. Does Aguilar sufficiently cover his tracks at Hooters?

5. How might differences in Spanish lead to disaster?

6. Do Nina's therapist and his counseling make sense?

7. Is the overall story and Nina's attitude biased and unfair to cats?

8. Why are cats so often associated with horror?

9. Is Nina a victim or a heroine? Both?

Chapter 8: *Il Noche de Fuego*

1. Do you accept that a jaguar can cause rocks to fall and an extinct volcano to seemingly erupt?
2. Are El Jefe's motives conflicted? How can he be a killer and a savior? Justify or refute the possibility.
3. The fact that the revelers on the Sandia Crest are oblivious to the horrific events occurring on the West Mesa involves a deliberate juxtaposition. Effective?
4. Does the early morning news account adequately resolve the tensions in the plot?
5. Is Tony, given his martial arts training, portrayed as too passive and ineffective throughout?
6. Is the news of Linda's illness as a kind of coda too contrived?
7. What is the story of La Lorona as related to Malinche?

Chapter 9: *Ella Vuelve*

1. Do you see the thematic appropriateness of different breeds mixing?
2. Can an animal be aware of its own heroism? How so?

3. Is Nina's return home consistent with her character?
4. Do you see a parallel in Nina's journey home to El Jefe's journey?
5. Is Raul's attitude toward coyotes that of a hunter, a rancher, or a conservationist? Do you see those roles as antithetical?

Epilogue: To end with the voice of El Jefe is fabulistic to be sure; however, is he entitled to his commentary? How so?